A Wishbone
Come True

Get your paws on the rest of the Puppy Powers series!

#1: A Wishbone Come True

#2: Wag, You're It!

Puppy Powers

A Wishbone Come True

BY KRISTIN EARHART
ILLUSTRATED BY VIVIENNE TO

Scholastic Inc.

To Talia — a talented pet trainer

ISBN 978-0-545-61759-8

12 11 10 9 8 7 6 5 4 3 2   14 15 16 17 18 19/0

Printed in the U.S.A.   40
First printing, January 2014

⭐ Chapter 1 ⭐

Lexi Torres raced on her bike through the town square. She didn't want to miss out on any fun. She slowed when she saw the dark storefront. Her heart dropped. Lexi was too far away to read the sign in the window, but she had a bad feeling. Had her brother been telling the truth?

Lexi hopped off her bike and walked it across the square. Her friends from the neighborhood were already there.

"What happened to Ms. Kidd?" Sadie

wondered. She tugged on her braid as she peered into the dark store.

"What happened to the toys?" added Max. The shelves were empty.

"Reed told me that there was a FOR RENT sign on the window," Lexi said, shaking her head. "I thought he was kidding."

"Kidding about the toy store being closed?" Henry asked. "That would be mean, even for your brother."

Lexi had to agree. She liked to look at things in terms of what was true and what was not true. It was easy to do with her brother. It was true that her brother liked a good joke. It was not true that he was mean.

Lexi sighed. Just that morning, Reed had put a plastic cockroach in her cereal. She would have preferred it the other way around: REAL cockroach, FAKE store closing.

"I guess we have to face it — Toys, Toys, Toys is really closed, closed, closed." Max kicked the toe of his sneaker against the front of the store. "I'm going to go to the park. Anyone else want to come with me?"

Lexi squinted at Max. How could he just go to the park? The four friends always spent Thursday afternoons with Ms. Kidd, the owner of Toys, Toys, Toys. Ms. Kidd sometimes set up archery tournaments for them, or she asked them to unpack boxes of the hottest new toys. She let them play with anything they wanted.

"I wonder if someone will open another toy store," Henry said.

"It can take a while to open something new," Sadie replied.

Nothing could compare to the toy store, but Lexi still hoped something else would open soon. The store was in the center of town. Four streets came together here, and there was a square in the middle with tall trees, a gazebo, and benches. The elementary school was on the other side of the square, and there was an ice cream store a few doors down.

"I have a football in my backpack. Let's just go to the park," Max said again. "Come on, Lexi. I'll bet Simon is there. He has soccer practice, right?"

"Max," Sadie said sharply. "Didn't you hear?"

Lexi bit her lip. She knew what Sadie was going to say. Lexi had been in a crummy mood before, but now she was all-out sad.

"What?" Max asked, looking from Sadie to Lexi and back to Sadie again.

"Simon is moving," Sadie explained. She had her left braid twisted into a tight knot now. "Like, next week."

"Oh. Sorry, Lexi," Max said.

"Yeah, sorry, Lexi," Henry added.

It was nice of them to apologize. It wasn't their fault that Lexi's best friend was moving away. Simon's dad just needed to live closer to his job.

Lexi had known Simon since they were, well, zero. They both loved scary books, bad jokes, and pumpkin ice cream. Simon and Lexi had done almost everything together. Everything except soccer. When Simon had soccer on Thursdays, Lexi had come to Toys, Toys, Toys with Henry, Sadie, and Max.

Now Simon was leaving the day before Lexi's birthday, two days before school started. They wouldn't do their homework together anymore. They wouldn't write spooky stories together. Simon wasn't even sticking around for Lexi's birthday party.

"It's okay," Lexi said. She turned to the store window again. She didn't want her friends to see the look on her face, but she could see herself in the window. Her whole face seemed to droop. Even her thick brown hair was limp today.

She was upset that Simon was moving, but Simon didn't seem sad at all. He had sounded excited when he told her, talking about the town's cool soccer field and the outdoor pool with a twisty slide. Lexi hadn't wanted Simon to see how sad she was, so she'd just made a joke.

Lexi reached up to trace her finger over the FOR RENT sign on the window. That's when she saw the light go on inside.

"Hey, guys," Lexi said. "I think someone's in there."

"Maybe it's Ms. Kidd," Henry said.

Lexi held her breath, but not a single person appeared. Instead a sturdy black cat strutted up the store's narrow aisle. A shaggy, caramel-colored dog plodded along behind her.

Lexi's heart began to pound when she saw the cat, and it melted when she saw the dog. She loved all animals, but dogs were her favorite.

"Oh, my gosh!" Sadie exclaimed. "They are so cute."

The cat walked straight up the aisle and leaped onto the desk where the cash register used to be. Her long, white whiskers twitched as she stared at the dog.

At once, the dog walked up to the window. Very carefully, he wedged his teeth between the glass and the FOR RENT sign.

He bit down and ripped the sign off the window. Then he ate it in five gigantic bites.

The cat blinked twice and jumped down. The two animals marched to the back of the store together. They were both wagging their tails.

⭐ Chapter 2 ⭐

"That's weird," Sadie said. "Cats don't usually wag their tails."

"Wait," Henry said, turning to his friend. "We just saw a cat and dog turn on a light. Then the dog ripped down a sign and ate it. And you're surprised that the cat wagged its tail?"

Lexi laughed.

Sadie dropped her braid and put her hands on her hips. "I'll have you know, I have read a lot about animals. It is extremely uncommon for a cat to wag its tail like that," Sadie said. "They usually only do it when they're mad. That cat looked pretty happy to me."

Lexi thought the cat and dog were adorable. She loved when cats and dogs were friends, and she didn't really care if the cat wagged its tail or not.

"Maybe a person is in there. Maybe the person flipped the light switch," Max insisted.

"Maybe the person is still there," Henry added.

At once, all four kids smashed together at the edge of the window. They stretched and strained, trying to see into the back of the store. Lexi just wanted to see the cat and dog again. She secretly hoped that they had turned on the light by themselves. She had read about pets that did amazing tricks. Some dogs could answer the phone or fetch their owners' slippers.

"Excuse me," said a low voice.

Lexi jumped. She was sure the others did, too. Still huddled against the window, they slowly turned and looked up. The owner of the voice had gray hair, and his eyes twinkled behind wire-rimmed glasses. He wore a checked shirt and a tan vest with lots of pouches and zippers. It looked like he was going fishing. But where had he come from? He couldn't have been in the store, or they would have seen him.

"I was just wondering if you like animals," he said. He was smiling. Lexi had a feeling he was laughing at them — in a nice way, like a big brother. "I thought you might, since you are staring into a pet store."

"Oh, yes. We all like animals," she answered. "We really like dogs. I mean, we don't just like dogs, we *love* dogs." Lexi was sure she could speak for her friends. They had all talked about wanting a dog.

"Oh, good," the man said. His funny grin spread into a wide smile. "I love dogs, too. All animals, really. My name is Mr. Power, and I am opening a pet store here. Did you see my sign?"

His sign? The four friends gave Mr. Power a good, long look. Max was the first to walk to the edge of the sidewalk. He looked up. "Hey, I didn't see that before."

The others joined him. Lexi was sure she would have noticed the turquoise-and-red sign on her bike ride through town. It said POWER'S PETS. How had it gotten there so fast?

"You should come back tomorrow with your parents," Mr. Power suggested. "It will be our grand opening. I'll have lots of pets for adoption. Puppies, too." Mr. Power seemed to look right at Lexi when he said it.

Puppies! Lexi felt chills all over her body.

Mr. Power smiled and started to turn away.

"Wait!" Max yelled, a little too loudly.

Mr. Power stopped. "Yes?" he asked.

"Were you just in the store?" Max asked.

"No, no," Mr. Power said. "I am just on my way in now."

Max paused. "Are the cat and dog yours?" he asked.

Mr. Power looked into the store. "Why, yes. Those two belong to me," he said. "Or maybe I belong to them. I can't be sure anymore."

"They turned on the light," Henry said quickly, "and then the dog ate the FOR RENT sign."

"Oh, no," Mr. Power mumbled and rubbed his chin. "What I really mean is, oh, yes. That sounds like them. Good pets with bad habits." He smiled. "If you come tomorrow, you can meet them. They're going to help me look after the shop."

With that, Mr. Power pulled a long loop of keys from a pouch in his vest. Lexi blinked. She thought she saw a tiny, whiskered nose stick its head out of one of the other pockets. Could it be a mouse?

"I hope you kids have a good day," Mr. Power said as he slipped a key into the store lock. "I've got a lot to do."

The kids all thanked him and said good-bye.

"We're headed to the park," Max announced. Henry was at his side.

"Okay, see ya," Lexi said with a wave. She didn't want to go to the park. She didn't want to see Simon and hear more about his cool new town.

Instead Lexi walked over to Sadie. She was still staring back at the store. It seemed like she was waiting for something. Just as Lexi glanced over, the dog appeared in the store window. He raised his fluffy paw as if he were waving. Without thinking, Lexi waved back.

⭐ Chapter 3 ⭐

Lexi shook the cereal box and scowled at her big brother, Reed. He always left four nuggets of granola in the box, instead of just finishing it.

Reed gave Lexi a crooked smile as she got up to make toast. "Have you made your birthday wish list yet?" he asked. "Is a puppy at the top again this year?"

Lexi decided to ignore him. Every birthday, Reed liked to remind Lexi that she didn't have a dog. Every Christmas, too.

In his own weird way, Reed was also reminding Mom and Dad that Lexi wanted a puppy. She had wanted a puppy ever since Simon got Bandit, an adorable black-and-white border collie. Bandit was like her adopted dog, but now Bandit was moving, too.

"Now, Reed." Mom often began speeches this way. "Pets are a big responsibility. . . ." Lexi had heard it all before. Her mom made a lot of speeches.

Lexi's mom talked a lot about why they *shouldn't* have a dog, but she had never said that they *couldn't ever* get a dog. This gave Lexi reason to hope, because a puppy would always be the first thing on her wish list.

"Now is not a good time to talk about it," their mom continued. "Lexi needs to stop by the school, so she can find out who her new teacher will be. Plus, Dad and I have a big trip to the hardware store planned."

Lexi looked over at Reed. He was stretching his arms out on both sides. He nodded at Lexi and mouthed the words, "Big trip to the hardware store. HUGE."

Lexi laughed into her hand. Reed didn't just make fun of Lexi; he made fun of *everyone*.

They did have a busy day ahead. Lexi was looking at the clock when the phone rang. She shoved the last bite of toast in her mouth and pushed back her seat. She rushed to the phone. "Hello," she said, hoping it was Simon.

"Hi, Lexi."

Lexi knew the voice at once. It was Simon's mom, Mrs. Stone. "Can I talk to Simon?" Lexi asked.

"He's busy right now, dear," Mrs. Stone said. "I'd like to talk to your mom."

Mrs. Stone did not sound like herself. Her words were short and stiff. They made Lexi feel hard inside. "Fine," Lexi mumbled as she pulled the phone away from her face. "I'm glad Simon's moving." She said it to herself, but she realized that Mrs. Stone had probably heard her, too. She looked up to see her mom staring at her. Lexi was not allowed to use that tone, especially not with adults. It was a Family Rule.

Mrs. Torres reached for the phone, and Lexi handed it to her. She half stomped out of the kitchen, but she stopped and peeked back around the corner.

Lexi listened to her mom's side of the conversation. She didn't say much. "I see," she said. "Yes," she agreed. "I understand," she said. "We'll see."

Lexi wished she could have talked to Simon. She was sorry that she had joked about his move.

Lexi held her breath when her mom hung up the phone. But her mom didn't come to find her. Instead she went to talk to Lexi's dad.

Lexi decided she'd take the chance to call Simon herself. She grabbed the phone and dialed.

"Hello?"

"Simon, it's me," Lexi said at once.

"Oh, hi." Simon's voice was flat. "I can't talk now, Lexi. Bye."

Lexi heard a click. Simon had hung up on her.

Half an hour later, Mr. Torres pulled into the school parking lot. Lexi looked across the square. Power's Pets was open now, and it looked crowded.

"It's time for the big photo!" her dad said as he opened her door. Every year, her parents took a picture of Lexi in the school courtyard.

Lexi gave her mom and dad a small smile, and then she walked up to the school. Mr. Butler, the principal, was sitting at a picnic table. He had a large box filled with envelopes in front of him. "Lexi Torres!" he called out. He knew each of his students by name. "I've got an envelope with your name on it. It's right here. In green ink." He flipped through the box, pulled out an envelope, and handed it to Lexi. "I was sorry to hear about Simon," he added.

"Thanks," Lexi said.

She shuffled over to where her dad was standing with the camera. She didn't even feel like opening the envelope. She knew Simon wouldn't be in her class.

"If you stand there," her dad said, "the light will be just right."

Lexi stood where her dad pointed.

"Smile, sweetie," her mom said.

Lexi held up the envelope and forced her mouth open so her teeth showed.

Just then, a breeze whipped through the school courtyard, lifting the envelope right out of her hand. Stunned, Lexi watched as the wind carried the envelope away. It twisted around a tree, made a giant loop across the square, soared over the gazebo — and zipped straight through the pet store's open front door.

★ Chapter 4 ★

"My envelope," Lexi whispered, staring at the door of Power's Pets. Something amazing had just happened. She was sure of it.

"What was that?" Lexi's dad asked.

"My envelope flew across the square and into the new pet store," Lexi explained.

"Sweetheart, envelopes don't fly. Be sure to say what you mean," Mrs. Torres advised. "How about you go get it while Dad and I go to the hardware store? We'll meet you out front," Mrs. Torres said.

Lexi's parents set off across the street, but Lexi lingered in front of the school. The air was calm now, so how did her envelope get all the way across the square? If Simon were there, he would agree that there was something strange about the whole thing.

Lexi crossed the street. When she got to Power's Pets, she gasped. The old toy store looked totally different. Yesterday, it had been empty. Today, it was full of animals and people.

As Lexi stepped inside, she saw a row of large cages lining one wall. They housed deluxe jungle gyms for hamsters, gerbils, and other tiny critters. Above Lexi's head, a jungle-green parrot perched on a swinging bar. There was a gigantic tank at the back of the store with bold red and electric-blue fish. The fish did loops and swirls together in perfect time. Three tabby kittens romped in a play area near the front window. The store felt festive, alive with happy chirps, squeaks, and chatter.

Lexi felt something cold and wet on her hand. She pulled her gaze from the kittens and looked down. There, at her feet, was the dog from the day before. He had something in his mouth. It was an envelope with her name written on it in green ink.

The dog sat down and looked up at Lexi with big brown eyes. His tail whipped back and forth in glee.

"He's excited to see you."

Lexi looked up. Mr. Power was walking toward her. He smiled. "Chance, I think you have something to give this young lady," he said. "Are you Lexi?" he asked, reading the name off her school envelope.

"Yes, I am," she said.

Chance whined and opened his mouth. Lexi took the envelope. "Thank you, Chance," she said, patting his head. "Where's your friend?"

"Oh, Lucky's watching the fish," Mr. Power explained. Lexi spotted the black cat sitting on top of the fish tank, staring down.

"Don't worry. Gus will make sure she keeps her paws to herself," the store's owner said with a smile.

Lexi looked more closely, and she saw a long-whiskered gray mouse plopped down next to the cat. She recognized him as the little mouse that had been in Mr. Power's pocket the day before.

"Welcome back to the store," Mr. Power said. "Would you like to meet a puppy?"

Mr. Power walked toward a large pen with a wooden gate. It was filled with shredded newspaper. Lexi saw lots of toys, but she didn't see a puppy.

Just then, a shiny black nose poked out from a pile of pillows. A fluffy puppy crawled out from under a red cushion. The puppy was mostly black with golden-brown markings above her eyes, across her chest, and on her legs. She gave herself a good shake, so her fuzzy fur puffed out even more.

"She's so cute!" Lexi said. It was true. She was the cutest puppy Lexi had ever seen.

Rrruff, ruff, the puppy barked. She trotted toward Lexi and put her front legs up on the side of the pen. *Rrruff, ruff!*

Lexi looked up at Mr. Power.

"I think she wants you to pick her up," he said.

Lexi quickly bent down and swooped the puppy into her arms. She was so soft! "Hey, you," Lexi whispered, and the puppy responded with a sloppy lick of Lexi's nose. Lexi giggled. As she pulled away, she noticed a shiny brass tag hanging from the puppy's collar. It read LUNA.

"Hi, Luna," Lexi said. "Is she the only puppy you have?"

"Well, yes. Right now. We aren't like most pet stores. We don't carry a lot of animals all of the time. We take animals who need a home, and we work to find the right family."

"Oh," Lexi said. He wouldn't let the puppy go home with just anyone. Lexi told herself it didn't matter. Her parents wouldn't let her have a puppy anyway.

Mr. Power walked away to help someone pick out cat food.

Luna wiggled and sniffed Lexi's neck. Lexi giggled and reached up to scratch the puppy. At once, Luna stopped squirming and her pink tongue fell out of the side of her mouth.

Lexi didn't even notice that Mr. Power had come back.

"You must have the magic touch," Mr. Power said. "Luna has a lot of energy. She doesn't calm down like that very often."

Lexi looked at the pet store owner. He sounded very serious.

He watched her thoughtfully. "Do you want to see her special trick?"

Of course Lexi did! She placed the puppy on the floor and waited.

That's when she heard her name. "Lexi! There you are!" It was her mom.

"Hey, sweetheart." And her dad.

Lexi took a deep breath, wondering if they would use that tone — the tone that meant she was in trouble. She was supposed to meet them on the sidewalk, but she had lost track of time.

"You must be Lexi's parents," Mr. Power said. He reached out and shook both of her parents' hands.

Lexi watched as her parents made small talk with the owner of the pet store. Luna jumped up and put her front paws on Lexi's leg. *Rrruff, ruff,* the puppy begged.

Lexi kneeled down. "I didn't mean to ignore you," she said. Lexi put both hands behind the puppy's ears and scratched. Immediately, the puppy's tongue dropped out the side of her mouth. It was so silly, Lexi had to laugh, but she also felt sad. She already loved Luna so much. She didn't want to say good-bye.

"Lexi, we need to head home," her mom reminded her.

Lexi looked at her mom with pleading eyes. She hadn't even seen Luna's trick yet!

"Before you go, could I show you Luna's special trick?" Mr. Power asked in a calm voice. "I promised Lexi I would."

It was as if Mr. Power had read her mind. Lexi looked hopefully at her parents. She crossed her fingers and held her breath.

⭐ Chapter 5 ⭐

"We can stay a bit longer," Mrs. Torres said to Mr. Power. Mr. Torres squeezed Lexi's shoulder.

"Great, you're going to love this trick!" Mr. Power said, kneeling down. He held up his finger to get the puppy's attention. Her bright eyes stared at the man's face. "Luna, sit."

The puppy tucked her back legs under her. Her ears pricked forward, but one of them flopped down. The pet store owner held up his finger again. "Luna, roll over three times," Mr. Power said, and he drew three circles in the air with his finger.

The puppy hunched down, pushed off, and did one perfect roll, followed by another. Halfway through the third roll, she stopped on her back and showed off her fuzzy brown belly.

"Come on, girl," Mr. Power encouraged her. "You can do it. This is important."

Still upside down, Luna turned her gaze from Mr. Power to Lexi. The puppy seemed to smile at her before finishing the third roll with a quick twist.

At once, Lexi felt something unexpected. Everything looked shimmery, as if sparkles were swimming all around her.

"What did you think?" Mr. Power asked quickly.

"She's the best," Lexi answered. She glanced up at her parents. They both looked dazed.

"You know what I think?" Mr. Torres blurted out.

"Yes, dear?" Mrs. Torres said.

"I think it's time for Lexi to get a dog."

"I was just thinking the same thing," Lexi's mom responded.

Lexi couldn't believe what she was hearing. She blinked several times, trying to clear the sparkles from her vision.

"Really?" Lexi asked.

"Yes, definitely," Mrs. Torres answered.

At that moment, Lexi heard a high, popping sound. The glitter effect immediately disappeared. Lexi's vision cleared again, and she realized Luna had crawled up into her lap.

"That's great news!" Mr. Power exclaimed. "I think Lexi will be an excellent dog owner. And what do you think about Luna? Is she the puppy for you?"

The puppy wiped her long, pink tongue across Lexi's chin.

"Oh, yes," Lexi said. "As long as my parents say it is okay."

Mr. and Mrs. Torres appeared stunned. "I can't believe I'm saying this, but I think Luna is the perfect puppy for you," Mrs. Torres said.

Luna's ears pricked forward at the sound of her name. She toddled out of Lexi's lap and nibbled at the strap on Mr. Torres's sport sandal.

"We'll have to get you some chew toys, Luna," Lexi's dad said.

Lexi couldn't stop grinning. It was really happening!

"Lexi," Mr. Power said, sounding serious again. "I need to show you how to get Luna to do her special trick." The store owner talked her through all the steps. He ended with the most important rule. "Luna should not do her special trick too many times. She's still a puppy. It will wear her out."

Lexi promised to follow all of the rules. She didn't want to do anything that would harm her puppy. *Her* puppy! It was still too good to be true. She couldn't wait to tell everyone about Luna. That's when the truth set in. She couldn't share her excitement with the one person she most wanted to tell, because that person wasn't talking to her.

Once they arrived home, Lexi was so full of glee she forgot about Simon. Luna was hilarious, darting around the house. She ran at full speed down the hallway and then stopped short to smell the sofa, and the newspaper, and a dirty sock.

"Oh, Luna," Lexi exclaimed. "That's Reed's sock. Gross."

"Is someone saying something mean about my socks?" Lexi's big brother came out of his bedroom, blinking in the sunlight-filled living room. "What? You got a dog?" Reed stared at the puppy in disbelief at first, then kneeled down and gave Luna a ferocious belly rub, wrapping his hands around her little body. The puppy dropped to the floor and rolled on her back for more.

"She really likes you," Lexi said.

"Everyone likes me," Reed said. Lexi rolled her eyes.

Mr. Torres walked in carrying a bag of brand-new dog toys. "That's so you don't chew on my shoes," he said in a stern tone to the puppy with the large, floppy ear. "Or my slippers," he added for good measure.

Luna trotted over to the pile of toys and began sniffing around. Lexi quickly started ripping open the packages and holding each one out for Luna to investigate.

Luna gave each toy a quick sniff and then seemed bored. The green-and-yellow braided rope. The blue bone. The squeaky turtle. All boring. She took off down the hallway again, her head bobbing up and down with each joyful stride.

Lexi stood up, ready to chase after her. Before she could follow the puppy down the hallway, Luna was back with a filthy tennis ball in her mouth.

"Give me that," Lexi insisted. "Come on, Luna."

Lexi grabbed at the ball and tugged, but Luna wouldn't let go. The puppy let out a playful growl. Her sharp white baby teeth dug into the ball.

"Come on, girl. Why don't you play with these other toys? How about this purple octopus?" Lexi begged.

"But she likes that one," Reed insisted.

Lexi couldn't believe it. Of all the toys in the house, why did she have to like that scuzzy old ball?

Lexi wanted her to drop it. She wanted her to play with something else. That old tennis ball belonged to Bandit, and it reminded Lexi of Simon all over again.

⭐ Chapter 6 ⭐

The next morning, Lexi awoke to Luna's happy *Rrruff, ruff, rufff.* The puppy's first bark was always extra long. It sounded like she was revving up. Luna was sitting next to Lexi's bed, her soft brown eyes focused on Lexi.

"Good morning, girl," Lexi said, half wondering if this was all still a dream. As soon as Lexi leaned over to pet the puppy, Luna stood on her hind paws and gave Lexi's hand a juicy lick. That warm, wet tongue felt real enough! The puppy's tail whipped back and forth. "I could get used to this," Lexi said and hurried out of bed. Luna ran in excited circles around her feet as she made her way to the kitchen.

"This is early for you," Lexi's mom said from her usual spot at the breakfast bar. "But your puppy's been awake for hours."

Lexi searched her mom's face. Was Luna already in trouble for being an early riser? Since it was the weekend, she guessed her dad and brother were still asleep. How long had her mom been up? "You can put her crate in my room, and then she won't wake you," Lexi suggested.

Luna, like many puppies, was trained to sleep in a special cage. Luna's crate was in a corner of the family room. She seemed to like her crate a lot. Mr. Power had explained that wild dogs used to take shelter in dens, and modern dogs still like to have a safe place to rest.

"She wasn't that much trouble," Lexi's mom said with a warm smile. "She kept me company while I did my yoga. Didn't you, girl?" Luna trotted over to the bar. She looked up at Mrs. Torres with her head tilted to one side.

Lexi smiled at the thought. She could picture her mom doing various stretches, and the puppy weaving herself around one posed leg, then the other. Lexi suspected Luna was very smart. The puppy knew that she needed to make friends with Mrs. Torres, and she had figured out just the way to do it.

Still, Lexi was worried. Something odd had happened at Power's Pets the day before. She didn't understand how her parents had changed their minds so quickly. That morning, her mom had declared that pets were too big a responsibility. Then, just a couple of hours later, she had said the opposite.

Lexi was concerned that her parents might change their minds again. She had waited so long for a puppy, and having Luna was even better than she had hoped. What if she had to take her back?

As Luna looked from Mrs. Torres to Lexi, her left ear flopped forward while her right ear stayed pricked. The puppy seemed to raise her eyebrows, trying to figure out what everyone was thinking.

"Luna was begging all morning, so I went ahead and fed her. She was so cute I couldn't take it," Mrs. Torres said. "But I think you should be in charge of feeding her from now on, Lex. It can be a new Family Rule." Of course! Lexi knew there would be lots of new Family Rules with a puppy in the house. Lexi also remembered that Mr. Power had given them a bunch of handouts on feeding and caring for a puppy. Lexi had been so excited, she had not read all the papers yet. But she already knew that puppies required special food.

"Did you know that puppies need twice the nutrients of full-grown dogs?" she asked her mom.

"I did," her mom responded. "It's because they are growing, just like kids." Mrs. Torres tousled Lexi's hair as she headed to the kitchen counter. "So don't you forget to eat, little lady. And give that puppy some water while you're at it."

Lexi gave her mom a quick, thankful hug. "You heard Mom," Lexi called to Luna, slapping her leg. "Let's get you a drink." The puppy bounded after Lexi, her tiny nails clacking against the tile floor. As soon as Lexi placed the full metal bowl next to the new food dish, the puppy plunged her black nose into the water and sneezed. Lexi attempted to resist the cuteness long enough to make toast.

Lexi had been so happy playing with Luna that she didn't remember the puppy's special trick until late afternoon, while she was talking to Reed.

Lexi was trying to learn all about her new teacher, Mr. Harvey. She had found a letter from Mr. Harvey inside the envelope that had magically flown into Power's Pets. "He sounds great," Lexi told her brother.

"Yeah, I had him," Reed said, "but that was *forever* ago."

"Come on, Reed," Lexi said. "It was only five years ago. You've got to remember something."

"Well, Mr. Harvey's the best, but he's not going to like you," Reed said in a typical, teasing tone.

"Why not?"

"Because he doesn't like students who do their homework, and raise their hands in class, and volunteer to help." Lexi's brother flashed his usual sly smile when he looked at her. "And he hates kids who bite their nails."

Lexi flinched and yanked her hand away from her mouth. Reed was, of course, describing her. Lexi scowled.

"Most important," Reed added, "is that he definitely doesn't like reports on dogs, the kind with lots of interesting canine facts."

"I don't think any of that is true," Lexi insisted. She was sure she remembered that

Mr. Harvey had a big Bernese mountain dog. She had seen him walking it on the other side of Castleton. And what teacher didn't like reports filled with facts?

"Believe what you want." Reed snorted and pretended to tune his guitar, but Lexi knew the guitar was missing a string. He wasn't going to play much of anything.

Sometimes it bugged her that her brother was always joking. She could never get a serious answer from him.

Lexi decided to ignore what Reed had said. She had written a lot of reports about dogs, and she wasn't going to stop now. If Mr. Harvey had them craft an essay on what they did over the summer, she would write about getting Luna. She knew she could write a good story about her fabulous new puppy. That's when she remembered Luna's trick.

"Want to see something?" she asked Reed. He shrugged.

Lexi took that as a yes. She knelt down and called Luna, trying to remember the right commands. The puppy trotted up to Lexi and sat down.

"Luna," Lexi said, holding up one finger. "Roll over three times." Then she made three circles in the air.

Luna's eyebrow whiskers went up, and she quickly got down on her haunches. Without a pause, the puppy rolled over once, twice, and a third time.

Lexi immediately gave Luna a treat. She was so happy that at

first she didn't notice the sparkles gathering in the air. The same thing had happened at the pet store, where everything had looked shinier than usual. Lexi glanced over at Reed, wondering if her big brother noticed anything unusual. Reed was staring straight at Lexi.

"Don't you just love her?" Lexi said, giving Luna a hug.

"Well, I guess so," Reed replied. "But not as much as I love you."

Lexi laughed through her nose. "What did you say?"

"I said that I love you." Reed's tone was earnest. "I know it's been hard with Simon moving. You know you can count on me, right?"

Reed stayed focused on her, his hazel eyes intent on her face.

"Um, thanks," Lexi said, trying to hide her smirk. She couldn't help it. Her brother was trying to be nice, and it was hilarious!

Reed was never funnier than when he was trying to be serious. She had to tell her mom!

"Mom!" She jumped up and bolted toward the kitchen with Luna at her heels. The sparkles seemed to follow them. "Mom! You'll never believe this," she yelled. "Reed told me he *loves* me." Lexi was out of breath when she arrived at the end of the long kitchen. The sparkles floated around the room, looking purple in the afternoon sun. She stopped just behind her mom. From the back, Lexi could tell her mom was cradling a bowl in one arm. In the other hand, she held a spoon.

When Mrs. Torres turned around, she had a guilty expression on her face.

"Mom, what are you doing?" Lexi asked. Lexi knew what it looked like — the mixer was out; flour dusted the counter-top. She could smell the cinnamon. Her mom was making cookies.

"Um," Mrs. Torres started. "I'm eating some cookie dough."

Lexi's jaw dropped. It was a Family Rule: No eating raw cookie dough! She had caught her mom in this same position before, with the bowl of dough held close to her side and the spoon nearly dangling from her mouth. Even when Lexi had asked, her mom had never admitted she was sneaking samples of unbaked yumminess before.

At that moment, Lexi heard a popping sound. It was just like the one she had heard in the pet store. The sparkles instantly disappeared, and her mom was still there with a sheepish half smile on her face.

Lexi had an odd feeling. Her skin tingled, and her mind was racing through all the possibilities. She was certain something was happening: sparkles, bizarre popping sounds, weird confessions. Lexi planned to figure out just what that something was. She was going to need Luna's help, but the puppy was already curled up in a tidy ball in her crate. Puppies needed their sleep, so Lexi would have to wait.

⭐ Chapter 7 ⭐

"Oh, Lexi," Sadie cooed. "You are just the luckiest. Luna is so sweet." Sadie sat cross-legged on the ground. The puppy was stumbling in and out of her lap, trying to nip at the red beads at the ends of Sadie's braids.

Lexi's face lit up with the smile of a proud parent. She was still so thrilled to be a pet owner, especially of a puppy like Luna.

"I can't believe your parents let you get a dog," Max said. "They won't even let you play in the sprinkler in your own backyard."

"My dad worries that a sprinkler is bad for the grass," Lexi explained. The Torres' yard was an even carpet of lush green grass. Her dad mowed it every weekend.

"Yeah, tell me about it," Max replied. His family owned a supersized water slide, and half the neighborhood hung out in their backyard during the summer. "Our grass is totally soggy and smashed, but a dog is a whole other story. A dog can ruin a yard."

"I'll bet your pooch came with a whole list of new Family Rules," Sadie added as she tried to dodge Luna's sloppy kisses. Lexi's friends had sometimes made fun of the Torres' many rules, but it didn't bug Lexi — not anymore.

"Well, that's kind of a good thing. I have a list. It helps me remember what I have to do to take care of her. The big rule is that I have to take her on walks, and I have to clean up after her. In the yard or wherever," Lexi told her friends. "And I can never let her pee on someone's trash cans, because Dad says that's disgusting and rude."

"He's right," Henry said. "That's one rule that makes sense."

Lexi laughed.

"Has Luna met Bandit yet?" Max asked.

Lexi shook her head. "I called Simon and left a message. I think they're out of town."

"No, I saw him at the park this morning," Max said.

This time, Lexi couldn't laugh it off. She had tried to call Simon yesterday and that morning. Why hadn't he called back? She didn't care if he wanted to brag all about how great his new town would be, she just wanted him to talk to her again.

She had been so upset last night after dinner she couldn't even eat pumpkin ice cream. Just seeing it in the freezer made her think of Simon. He was the only other person she knew who even liked pumpkin ice cream.

She didn't understand why Simon was avoiding her. Shouldn't they be trying to spend time together before he moved? Was he so excited about his new house and new town that he didn't want to hang out with her anymore?

As if Henry knew what she was thinking, he changed the subject. "Can Luna do any tricks?" he asked. He was snapping his fingers, trying to get her to beg.

"She can," Lexi answered. She focused on her playful puppy. "Luna can already beg, shake hands, sit, and fetch. Here, I'll show you." But Lexi wasn't going to show her friends the puppy's special trick yet.

She had a plan for when to unleash that trick next, and she needed to save up all of Luna's energy for it to work.

That afternoon, after her mom came home, Lexi decided it was time to test out Luna's trick again. Luna had had a long nap, and they were all in the backyard. Lexi's mom was cutting back the rose-bush. The scent of the late-summer blooms sweetened the air.

Lexi plopped herself down close to where her mom was working. Luna trotted over and nudged Lexi for a pet. Lexi reached out with both hands and scratched the puppy behind her velvety ears.

"Hey, Mom?" Lexi asked. "Can I ask you something?"

"Sure, honey," her mom responded between snips of the garden shears.

"Do you know why Simon is mad at me?"

"People don't get mad, Lexi. Animals get mad," her mom said. "People get angry."

Her mom was avoiding the question.

"Do you know why Simon is angry with me?" Lexi tried again.

"Is he angry with you? I really don't think he is, Lex." A sadness tugged on the corners of her mom's mouth. Lexi could tell her mom wasn't telling her something. She was holding back. Lexi needed to put the plan into action.

Lexi took a deep breath, held up one finger, and told Luna to sit. Next, she made three perfect circles in the air with her finger and asked the puppy to roll over three times. Luna gave a happy yip and then quickly did a triple roll, flashing her light-brown belly with each turn. As soon as Luna was finished, sparkles filled the air. They glittered all around Lexi, Luna, and Mrs. Torres.

"Mom," Lexi began, feeling a little nervous. "How do you know Simon isn't angry with me?"

"Because his mom would have told me."

Lexi paused. She wanted to ask the right question. "Well, what did she tell you? What did you and Mrs. Stone talk about on the phone?"

Mrs. Torres took a deep breath, and then the words came rushing out. "Oh, Lexi. I wanted to tell you, but Kate made me promise not to."

Lexi knew that Kate was Simon's mom's first name. The two moms were friends.

"Simon didn't want you to know, but he asked his mom to call me," her mom continued. "He thought she could convince me to let you have a dog for your birthday." Lexi's mom had dropped her garden clippers and was gazing right into Lexi's eyes.

"Getting a puppy was Simon's idea?"

Her mom nodded.

"But why?"

"He thought you would like one. He said it might keep you from missing him and Bandit."

Lexi listened, trying to take it all in. She didn't know how long it would last — this crazy sparkly effect — but she wanted to make the most of it. She wanted to get as much information as possible.

"Is there anything else you want to tell me?" Lexi asked.

Her mom paused. "Yes, sweetheart. I really wish you'd wear those barrettes I got for you. Your hair is always in your eyes."

"What?" Lexi couldn't believe that in the middle of a heart-to-heart discussion, her mom wanted to discuss her hairstyle. "No, Mom, is there anything else about Simon?" Lexi still didn't understand why Simon would suggest that her parents get her a dog if he was mad at her. He had to be mad — or angry — at her. Why else wouldn't he call back?

"Well, there is something," Mrs. Torres began. "I really wanted Simon to tell you, but —" She was in the middle of her thought when there was a *pop*. She immediately stopped.

The sparkles disappeared. Mrs. Torres had that look again, the one she had after she ate the cookie dough.

"What is it, Mom? I still don't get it," Lexi said. "Why won't he talk to me?"

"Oh, Lexi. Kate asked me not to talk to you about any of this." Mrs. Torres sounded more like herself again. Her words were more clear, more even. "It's really Simon's place to tell you." Her mom reached forward and gently tucked a strand of loose hair behind Lexi's ear. "Lex, you need to talk to Simon. I'm sure you'll find a way."

Lexi wasn't sure how she would get Simon to talk to her. Even if she could, she didn't know if she could fix their friendship. It was true that they were best friends, but they had never really talked about feelings. They talked about dogs, books, and gross jokes.

Lexi was so deep in thought, she almost forgot about Luna. The puppy sniffed at Lexi's foot and licked her toe.

"Are you trying to tell me something, girl?" Lexi asked, stroking the puppy's back. "I'll bet you want to help," she said to her puppy. Lexi didn't know how or why, but she was certain that Luna's special trick wasn't just special. It was *magic*. Every time the puppy did a triple roll, the sparkles appeared. Every time the sparkles appeared, people told the truth.

"Let's do your trick one more time, Luna," Lexi said. She hoped that it was just what she needed to make things with Simon good again.

⭐ Chapter 8 ⭐

After a lot of thinking, Lexi had figured out a plan. If Simon wouldn't answer her calls, she would have to track him down. She picked up Luna's red leash and gave it a shake. "Luna," she called. Lexi could hear the *jangle, jangle, jangle* of the puppy's collar before she rounded the corner from the hallway.

Rrruff, ruff. Luna jumped up on Lexi when she saw the leash.

"Hey, girl," Lexi said. "Let's go for a walk. I want you to meet someone."

A little while later, Lexi and Luna arrived at the corner of Clearview and Evening Streets. Lexi checked her watch. She knew Simon really well. It was true that Simon was often late for school, soccer, dinner, and sleepovers. But he was never late for walking Bandit. He was always on time, and he always took his border collie on the same route. Lexi was counting on that.

"He'll be here, Luna, I'm sure of it. You just have to be ready," Lexi advised. Luna sat patiently and kept watch.

After they had been waiting for ten minutes, Luna looked up at her owner with deep brown eyes. The puppy let out a few hopeful whines. "We have to have faith, girl," Lexi said, but she was worried, too. Had Simon changed his route? Had he seen Lexi and gone the other way?

"We didn't miss them, Luna," Lexi

assured her puppy. "If they turned onto this street, we would have seen him."

Just then, Lexi saw a familiar black-and-white head poke out from behind a house. Next came the loose, two-legged stride she knew so well. It was Bandit and Simon, side by side. Luna's eyebrows shot up and she made three happy barks. "Shhh, Luna," Lexi pleaded, but it was too late. Lexi could see Simon pause.

"That's not fair," Lexi grumbled. "He has to come."

Luna butted her head against Lexi's leg. The puppy whimpered and gazed at Lexi with big, white-rimmed eyes. Looking at Luna, Lexi remembered their plan. "You're right. Let's just do the trick. Right now."

"Hey, Simon!" Lexi yelled. "Come here, I want to show you something."

Even from far away, Lexi could tell he was hesitating. *Rrruff*, the puppy yipped.

Lexi knelt down. "Luna, please help me talk to Simon." Lexi took a deep breath and asked Luna to roll over three times. Then Lexi made the three circles in the air.

Luna had never rolled over so fast! Within seconds, the puppy was finishing her final twist. She hopped back up, her tongue dangling out of the side of her mouth.

As soon as Lexi saw the sparkles, she started talking, nice and loud. "Simon!

Thank you for telling my parents to let me have a dog. It worked!" As Lexi kept speaking, Simon slowly walked toward her. "It was so nice of you, especially since you're mad at me."

Simon and Bandit stopped when they were about ten feet away.

"I'm not mad at you," Simon said. "I thought you were mad at me! You know, for moving." The two best friends faced each other, and the sparkles seemed to

float all around them. Lexi had no idea how Luna's magic worked, but the sparkles made it easier to say exactly what was on her mind.

"It's not your fault that you're moving. I wish you weren't. It's weird thinking about you living somewhere else and doing fun new things without me." Lexi paused. "And now I have a puppy, and it will be weird doing dog things here without you."

"I wish I could stay," Simon said.

"You do? But you sounded so excited," Lexi said, feeling confused. "I thought you were really happy about moving."

Simon glanced up at Lexi. "No. I was really bummed, so my mom told me to think about the good things. That's why I told you about the pool and that stuff. I was just trying to make it sound cool."

Lexi felt a rush of relief. Simon wasn't looking forward to moving away and leaving her! But that didn't explain everything. She needed more answers.

"I don't get it. Why didn't you call me back?"

"I didn't know what to say. I didn't want you feeling bad for me, but I didn't want to lie about liking the new place either."

Lexi let Simon's words sink in. She had been relieved that Simon wasn't happy about moving, but that also meant that Simon wasn't happy. She wanted to try to help. "Your new house sounds nice. I bet you'll like it. And you'll make lots of new friends."

Simon shrugged.

"Maybe they'll even like pumpkin ice cream," Lexi added hopefully.

"Maybe," Simon said.

Lexi heard the familiar *pop*. The magic was over. She wondered if Simon would stop talking to her now. Without the spar-kles, she didn't know what to say.

Lexi took a deep breath. "I'll miss you," she said. She realized that she had been thinking about how much she'd miss Simon, but she had never told him.

"I'll miss you, too," Simon replied. "When I was really sad, Bandit made me feel better. That's how I got the idea that you needed a dog, too."

"Thanks, Simon. That was super nice of you." Suddenly, Lexi felt like she had her best friend back. "I'm sorry you're not excited to move. But I'm glad you're talk-ing to me again."

"Yeah. Talking with you is okay, but I really just wanted to meet your puppy," Simon joked. "She's really cute. What's her name?"

"Luna," Lexi replied. "Look, she wants to meet Bandit." Luna was bowing down, her tail wagging high in the air. She pulled on the leash. She barked. She barked again. "Can we introduce them?"

"Let's walk and see how they get along," Simon suggested. They all headed toward town. Simon told Lexi about training Bandit as a puppy. The two dogs padded along next to each other, tongues long and tails curled.

"Do you think they like each other?" Lexi asked.

"I think so," Simon said. "Bandit likes to feel in charge, so he likes younger dogs." As the dogs marched along, Luna kept glancing up at the older dog.

Lexi could not believe how normal it seemed, walking Luna alongside Simon and Bandit.

It *was* very normal, until a not-very-normal wind blew down the street. It was a warm, tingly wind. It was a wind a lot like the one that had lifted the envelope out of her hands a few days earlier.

This gust seemed to have a mind of its own. The swift air swirled in and lifted the leashes out of both Simon's and Lexi's hands. As if on cue, Bandit and Luna took off at a full gallop, the leashes carried on a gust of air behind them. The dogs yipped playfully and bounded ahead. Taken by surprise, Simon and Lexi stood and watched in a daze. Then, all at once, they realized their dogs were running away!

⭐ Chapter 9 ⭐

"What happened?" Simon blurted out as he and Lexi took off after their dogs. "Where are they going?"

"I don't know," Lexi answered. The soles of her shoes slapped against the hard sidewalk. The dogs were almost a full block ahead, and they were headed straight toward the center of town.

The wind kept blowing, pasting wisps of hair across Lexi's face. The dogs were racing down a busy street. It was dangerous!

Lexi trusted that dependable Bandit would look out for her puppy.

As they neared Castleton Elementary, Lexi spotted the two dogs running across the street into the town square. Luna and Bandit paused in the center and looked back at Simon and Lexi, as if they were making sure their owners were still following them.

"Bandit, wait!" Simon yelled. "Stay there, boy."

Lexi stared across the street. She was afraid to call to Luna. What if the puppy ran across the street toward Lexi? What if there was a car?

Lexi and Simon watched the crosswalk sign. As soon as the signal changed, they darted across the street. When they were halfway there, Luna and Bandit took off toward the far end of the square. They bounded across Main Street and trotted straight into Power's Pets. "I feel like this has happened before," Lexi said under her breath.

The next crosswalk signal changed, and the pet owners rushed to the opposite sidewalk and into the pet store. There, Luna and Bandit were slurping up water from two bowls. It looked like someone had set out the water in anticipation of two runaway dogs.

"Well, there you are," Mr. Power said

upon seeing Lexi and Simon. "I knew you couldn't be far."

For a moment, Lexi worried that Mr. Power would be angry with her. After all, no one should let a puppy run loose around town! But Mr. Power didn't seem concerned. Lexi rushed forward and swooped her puppy up in her arms, and then buried her face in Luna's soft belly.

"Don't you do that again, Luna," Lexi demanded, even though she knew it wasn't the puppy's fault.

"Quite a wind out there today, isn't it?" Mr. Power said.

"It is," Simon agreed. He sat on the floor next to Bandit, and the dog rested his chin on Simon's leg. The dogs seemed so calm now. It was hard to believe that they had just gone on a wild chase across the town.

Lexi studied the pet store owner. He was wearing the same vest as before — and the same knowing smile.

"You thirsty?" he asked, offering them glasses of water.

"You bet," Simon said, taking one.

Lexi reached out for a glass as well. It seemed as if Mr. Power had been expecting them.

"You know, I think I'll need some helpers around the shop," Mr. Power said. "The previous toy store owner mentioned that you and your friends might be up for the job."

"Really, Ms. Kidd said that?" Lexi asked.

"Sure. Maybe you want to come by on Thursday afternoons to help walk dogs and play with the animals?"

Lexi thought of Henry, Max, and Sadie. "I'd love that," she exclaimed. "So would my friends. I'll ask them for sure." She was excited just thinking about it.

"And what about you?"

It took Simon a moment to realize that Mr. Power was talking to him. "Oh, me?" Simon said. "I'm moving, so I guess I won't be able to help out."

Now that Lexi knew the truth, she could see it all over Simon's face. Even if his new town had great soccer fields and a huge pool, he was still sad to move. He had never helped out at Toys, Toys, Toys, but Lexi suspected he would have been there every week if the store had been Pets, Pets, Pets.

"I see," Mr. Power said. "Well, you'd still be welcome. Maybe when you come back to visit."

Lexi looked outside. Through the large picture window, she could see that the trees were now perfectly still. No leaves rustled. The air was calm again. It was odd how that crazy wind had just gone away.

"Where are you moving, son?" Mr. Power asked.

"Ashland," Simon answered, his voice low. He buried his hand in the long hair around Bandit's neck.

"That's not so far," Mr. Power said. "It's just on the other side of Carmel. Did you know that Carmel has a great new dog park? It's only about twenty minutes from here."

It took Lexi a minute to figure out what Mr. Power was saying.

"Wait, Simon, do you think your parents would drive you and Bandit to the dog park in Carmel?" Lexi asked. "To see Luna and me?"

Simon slowly looked up at Lexi. A smile spread across his face. "I know they would. They keep saying that we aren't moving that far, and that we can come back to visit," Simon said. He gave Bandit's back a long pet.

"I can get a ride, too," Lexi said. "I'm sure of it."

Lexi set Luna down, and the puppy toddled over to Bandit. The two dogs smelled each other's noses, and Luna nuzzled up against Bandit's belly to rest. They looked like they'd been buddies forever.

"Maybe we can try to meet up on weekends," Simon said. "Then our parents can talk, too."

Lexi knew her parents would like that. They would miss Simon and his family, too.

While Lexi was standing there, she felt something cold and wet on her hand. She knew at once it was Chance, Mr. Power's dog. With a quick survey of the room, she located Lucky, the cat that lived in the pet store. Lucky looked to be asleep on top of the food shelf, but she was watching everyone out of a half-opened eye. Peeking out from under her tail was Gus, the fearless mouse. There was definitely something odd about Power's Pets, but in a good way. "And I think you should try to come help in the store sometimes," Lexi added. "I know Max, Henry, and Sadie will want to see you."

"That would be great," Simon said.

"I could sure use the extra hands," Mr. Power said. "There's a lot to keep track of around here. We're getting some special new puppies in early next week."

Lexi knew that the puppies could not be as special as Luna — could they? She wondered if the new puppies might do amazing tricks, too.

"We should head out now," Simon suggested. "I think your pup needs a nap soon."

Luna opened her jaws into a wide yawn and her long tongue rolled out.

"You're right," Lexi agreed, "but maybe we can get an ice cream on the way home?"

"Sounds good," Simon said, sounding thoughtful.

As they left the store, Lexi turned back to wave. Mr. Power and Chance both smiled at her. Lexi looked forward to the next time she'd be back, but she had a busy week ahead. Simon had a lot to teach her about dog training before he left.

"You know," Simon started, "I feel like we did a good job earlier telling each other the truth."

"Yeah," Lexi agreed.

"So I need to tell you something else."

Lexi gulped. Luna hadn't done her trick. There weren't any sparkles in the air. What did Simon have to say?

"Lexi, I've wanted to tell you this for a while." Simon took a deep breath. "Pumpkin

isn't my favorite ice cream flavor anymore. It's vanilla."

"What? Vanilla? Are you kidding me?" Lexi exclaimed. "I don't know if I can be best friends with someone whose favorite flavor is vanilla!" Lexi looked at Simon and laughed. It felt good to have her best friend back.

Sure, he was moving and that would change some things. But it didn't always take magic to know the truth. Lexi knew that she and Simon would always be great friends. And their dogs would, too.

More Puppy Powers!

PET HOTEL

Look who's checking in
at the Pet Hotel!

PET HOTEL
Calling All Pets!

KATE FINCH · SCHOLASTIC

PET HOTEL
A Big Surprise

KATE FINCH · SCHOLASTIC

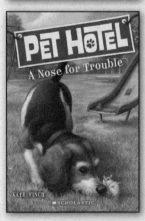

PET HOTEL
A Nose for Trouble

KATE FINCH · SCHOLASTIC

PET HOTEL
On with the Show!

KATE FINCH · SCHOLASTIC

WHERE EVERY PUPPY FINDS A HOME

 MUTTLEY

 ZIGGY

 BELLA

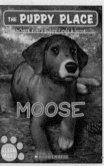 MOOSE

 BANDIT

 COCOA

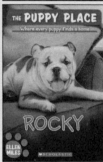 ROCKY

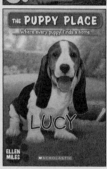 LUCY

 TEDDY

 MOCHA

 OSCAR

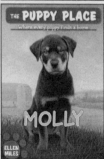 MOLLY

The Rescue Princesses

These are no ordinary princesses—
they're Rescue Princesses!